# The Adventures of Swashbuckle Lil

## A pirate's life!

'Rip-roaring rhyming text interspersed on every page by lively, wacky black-and-white illustrations . . . a book that will make young readers chuckle and giggle' *Carousel* magazine

'The rhyming text and detailed drawings provide guidance and encouragement to youngsters transitioning from supervised to independent reading. Imaginative, witty, entertaining and lots of fun' BookTrust

'Anderson's illustrations burst with energy and humour' *Bookseller*

'Told in jolly rhyme that makes reading the stories particularly fun and easy, and with lively black-and-white illustrations on every page, these are the perfect step up from picture books to chapter books' lovereading4kids.co.uk

'Just as _____ l – the illu_____ the classic _____ bag

*By Elli Woollard for younger readers*
*from Macmillan*

Rudyard Kipling's Just So Stories
The Giant of Jum
The Dragon and the Nibblesome Knight
The Great Gran Plan

# ELLI WOOLLARD

## The Adventures of

# Swashbuckle Lil

## A pirate's life!

ILLUSTRATED BY LAURA ELLEN ANDERSON

MACMILLAN CHILDREN'S BOOKS

First published 2016 and 2017 in two separate volumes as
*Swashbuckle Lil: The Secret Pirate* and *Swashbuckle Lil and the Jewel Thief*
by Macmillan Children's Books

This edition published 2018 by Macmillan Children's Books
an imprint of Pan Macmillan
20 New Wharf Road, London N1 9RR
Associated companies throughout the world
www.panmacmillan.com

ISBN 978-1-5098-8152-9

A CIP catalogue record for this book is available from
the British Library

Printed and bound by CPI Group (UK) Ltd, Croydon CR0 4YY

# Contents

# The Secret Pirate

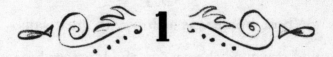

When Lil sat at school doing spellings and sums,

Nobody, nobody guessed

That she wasn't at all like an ordinary girl,

And that under her jumper and vest . . .

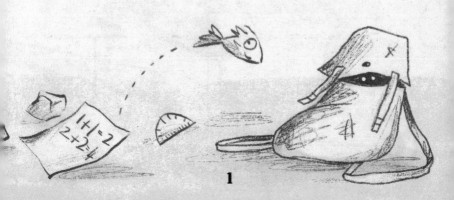

# Lil was a pirate, a swashbuckling pirate,

Whose home was a ship with great sails,

Who had travelled the seas in the blustery breeze

And had ridden the waves with huge whales.

2

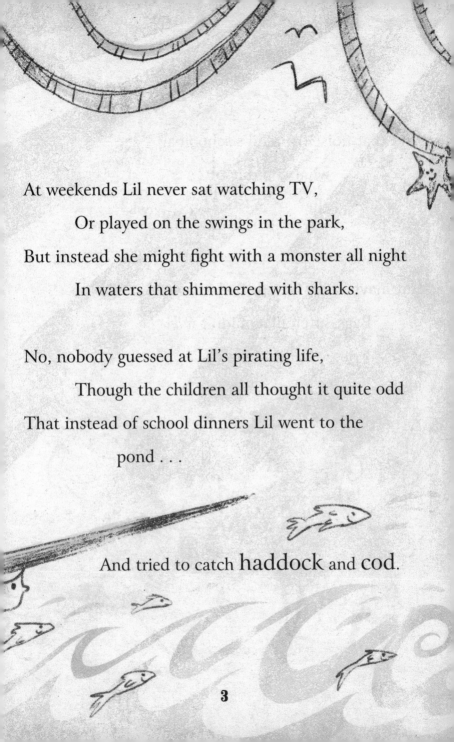

At weekends Lil never sat watching TV,

     Or played on the swings in the park,

But instead she might fight with a monster all night

     In waters that shimmered with sharks.

No, nobody guessed at Lil's pirating life,

     Though the children all thought it quite odd

That instead of school dinners Lil went to the

     pond . . .

And tried to catch haddock and cod.

And that noise from Lil's schoolbag –

what could it be?

A shuffle? A rustle? A squawk?

But maybe Lil's friends had imagined it all;

Bags, after all, couldn't *talk*!

Sometimes Lil simply forgot where she was

As she sat gazing out at the sky,

And then, when her teacher, Miss Lubber, said, 'Lil?'

She'd shout out, **'Ahoy!'** in reply.

'Lil,' said Miss Lubber, 'stop daydreaming, please!

Remember you're here to learn facts!

Pirates aren't real! It's time now, I feel,

That you learned how a good schoolchild acts.'

Lil hated to sit on her bum all day long.

Her school seemed most desperately dull.

But one day some paper appeared on her desk,

And on it . . .

the Sign of

the Skull!

Lil shivered and shook as she thought to herself,

'We've trouble ahead, there's no doubt!

I know who drew *that* (oh, the rotten old rat!),

Yes, the terrible Stinkbeard's about!'

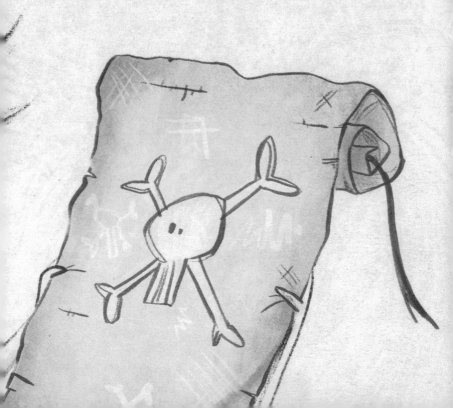

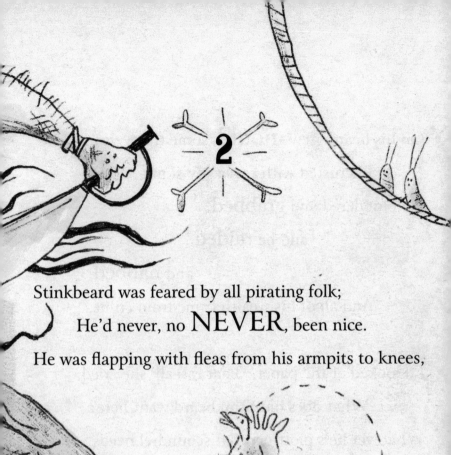

# 2

Stinkbeard was feared by all pirating folk;

He'd never, no **NEVER**, been nice.

He was flapping with fleas from his armpits to knees,

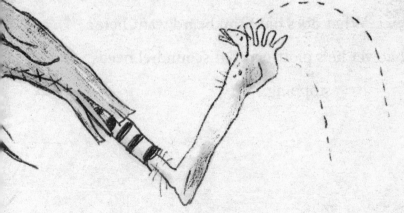

And even his toenails had lice.

On his beard grew mould, some thirty years old,

    Encrusted with seaweedy slime.

He plundered and grabbed,

       and he raided

              and nabbed,

    And all of his wealth came from crime.


Lil looked at the paper. 'That rascal!' she cried,

    'What does old Stinkbeard want here?

Whatever he's plotting, that scoundrel needs

    stopping.

    *That* much is perfectly clear.'

'Miss Lubber!' Lil shouted. 'Ahoy! Look outside!

There's a wicked old pirating guy!'

But her teacher said, 'Lil, just be quiet and sit still!

There *aren't* wicked pirates – don't lie!'

At playtime Miss Lubber said, 'Lil, stay inside!

Write "Children must all tell the truth".'

Lil whispered to Carrot, her trusty red parrot,

'Find Stinkbeard, and then be my sleuth.

'That rotten old rat always talks to himself.

He mutters and mumbles all day.

So go and find out what he's talking about.

We won't let that brute get away!'

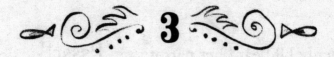

**3**

Lil waited and waited for Carrot's return;

The minutes were ticking away.

Could Stinkbeard be found? Was he even around?

And what was he likely to say?

Stinkbeard was known for his dastardly deeds.

He'd even once burgled a bank!

What would he do? Snatch Year Two as his crew?

Or yell, 'Year One, walk the *plank*'?

Suddenly Lil heard her parrot say, 'Pssst!'

But Miss Lubber came up, with a frown.

'This is no time for fun; there is work to be done!

Break-time is over!
# Sit down!'

What could Lil do? She must go outside,

    Yet Miss Lubber was sure to refuse.

She had to make haste. There was no time to waste,

    Not one single moment to lose.

'Miss!' Lil yelled. 'There's a wasp in the room!

Or some kind of hornet or bee!

Look! Over here!

Over there! On that chair!

There's another one now – can't you see?'

The class started screaming and

screeching and shrieking

(One little boy even cried),

And as they all fled from imaginary bees . . .

Lil slipped unnoticed outside.

'Pieces of eight!' squawked Carrot the Parrot.

'Hurry up, Lil – we must dash!

That Stinkbeard is planning to kidnap Miss Lubber,

Then ask for a ransom in cash!'

'To the rescue!' Lil shouted to Carrot the Parrot.

'Now where's Stinkbeard lurking?' she said.

'We can't let that **creature**

get hold of my **teacher!**'

But Carrot just scratched at his head.

Lil se$_a$rch$^e$d

and she sn$_i$ff$_e$d,

and she sn$_i$ff$_e$d

and she se$_a$rch$^e$d.

'He's somewhere around, I can tell.

But just as I'd feared, he's quite disappeared!

Quickly now – follow that smell!'

In all of the places that Stinkbeard had been,

A horrible **pong** filled the air.

Lil bravely went on, but it seemed he had gone;

That scoundrelly scum wasn't there!

But whose was that shadow

so sneakily snaking?

It had to be Stinkbeard at last!

'Now,' whispered Lil, 'I must get him, but how?

I'll have to be ever so fast!'

Lil grabbed at the ropes from some children

out skipping.

'Oi!' they all shouted. 'Don't snatch!'

But Lil said, 'I'll borrow them, just till tomorrow,

Right now, there's a pirate to catch!'

'**A**rrrrrgh!'
    shouted Lil as she leaped in the air
And tied up old Stinkbeard with rope.
'You won't get away if you try for a day!
    Don't struggle – you've not got a hope.'

But all of a sudden the man turned right round.

What horror! Oh, what a disaster!

It was not, as Lil thought, old Stinkbeard

she'd caught,

Instead she had got . . .

the Headmaster!

'Oops!' muttered Lil. 'Just a little mistake.

   Really quite easily done.

But if you don't mind, I've a pirate to find,

   So now, I'm afraid, I must . . . RUN!'

# 5

There was no time to think. Lil raced up a tree

As fast as she could, at the double.

The Headmaster was fuming, and furiously

# BOOMING:

'Young Lil, you're in terrible trouble!'

But wait. What was that – up overhead?

Lil parted the leaves and she peered.

The *thing* was all bristly and grimy and gristly;

It wasn't a bird, but a . . .

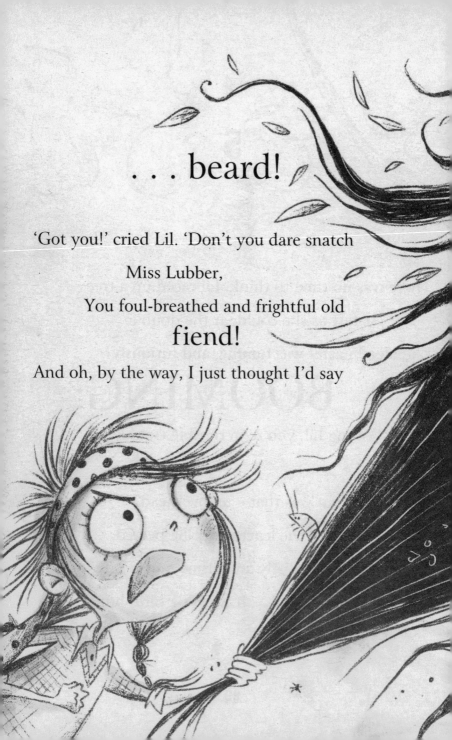

# . . . beard!

'Got you!' cried Lil. 'Don't you dare snatch

Miss Lubber,

You foul-breathed and frightful old

## fiend!

And oh, by the way, I just thought I'd say

Your abominable beard should be

# cleaned.'

Stinkbeard gave Lil the most gruesome great grin

As he narrowed his mean little eyes.

'A girlie? How cute! You'd be lovely as loot,

I will take you away as my prize!'

'Never!' Lil yelled. 'Get out of my school,

You vicious and villainous man!

You think that you'll snatch me?

Come on then – c a t c h   m e !

Just try it and see if you can.'

With a cry of, 'Avast!' Lil leaped from the tree

(A trampoline stood right below).

She bounced in the air, and right then and there

Turned somersaults, three in a row.

Lil raced through the playground, she raced

through the school.

Stinkbeard was hot on her heels.

'The thing that I need,' Lil said, 'is more speed.

I know – I'll have to use . . .

# wheels!'

The lunch cart was laden with food for school dinner;

With pizzas and salads and cakes.

Lil tore through the rooms.

How she zipped!

How she zoomed!

But then Carrot squawked,

'**Help!** There aren't brakes!'

With a crash and a smash and a clatter and clash,

The trolley went *wham!* in the wall.

All the shelves full of books,

all the coats on their hooks,

*Everything* started to fall.

There was nowhere to run,

there was nowhere to hide,

As Stinkbeard yelled, 'Got you, young creature!

Whatever you say, you won't get away.

And now, I will kidnap your teacher.'

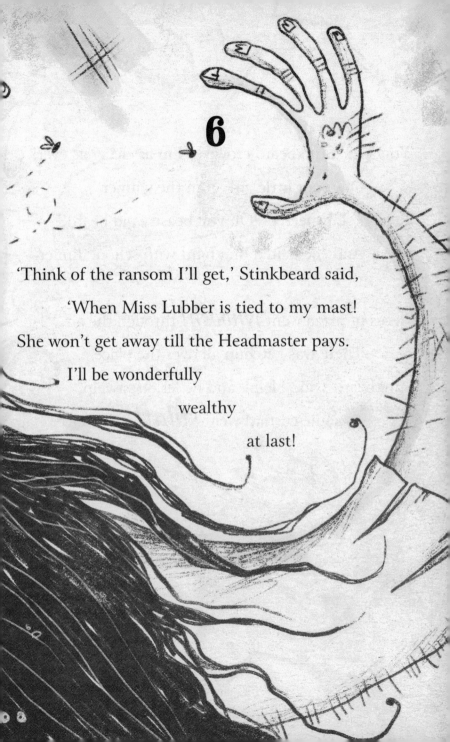

**6**

'Think of the ransom I'll get,' Stinkbeard said,

'When Miss Lubber is tied to my mast!

She won't get away till the Headmaster pays.

I'll be wonderfully

wealthy

at last!

'You see?' Stinkbeard crowed, 'I'm as clever as ever!

   Oh, poor little girl – I'm the winner!'

'Really?' Lil sneered. 'Oh you beastly old beard!'

   And she pelted him hard with school dinner.


Pieces of pizza went *whoosh!* through the air,

   There was ketchup all over the place.

Stinkbeard said, 'Help!' and he let out a yelp,

   As some custard went *splat!* in his face.

Gravy oozed down from the top of his head,

Eggs went *ker-splot!* in his eyes.

'Just let me be!' Stinkbeard yelled, 'I can't see!

I'm covered in burgers and fries!'

'Promise you won't snatch Miss Lubber,' said Lil,

'You scurvy old scoundrelly scum!'

Then just as he fled, down Carrot sped

And bit Stinkbeard – peck-peck – on the bum.


'Phew!' said Lil. 'Good riddance, at last.

Now I think that I might have a nap.'

But then she bent down, and she said, with a frown,

'Oh look! Stinkbeard's dropped this old map!

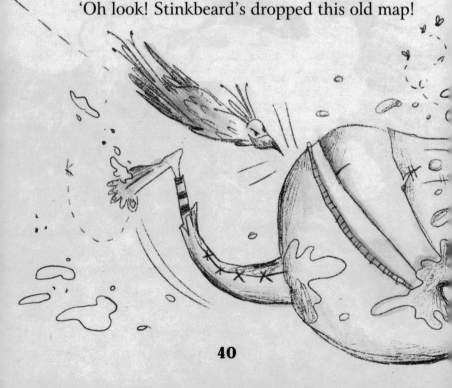

'Treasure!' Lil cried. 'And X marks the spot!

Let's hope that we find something big.

It's outside, by the roses (where no one supposes),

Come on then, Carrot – let's dig!'

Lil dug at the flowers for what seemed like hours,

    Then she came to a barrel marked TREATS.

And she said to her parrot, 'Let's party, me hearty,

    This treasure chest's chock-full of sweets!'

But whose were those footsteps, *thumpety-thump*,

    Approaching Lil over the grass?

Miss Lubber! Bright red, as she furiously said,

    'Detention! Now get back to class!'

'But I saved you,' cried Lil,

'from a fate worse than death!'

Miss Lubber said, 'No, you're just naughty.

Now sit over there and don't move from that chair.

And tell me, what's twenty

plus forty?'

'Huh!' muttered Lil as she stomped to her desk,

'Miss Lubber is really the worst!

If I wasn't so nice I might give some advice

And say she *deserved* to be cursed!

'But I am a pirate, a good sort of pirate,

And when there is someone to save,

Then I'll do what is right (if it takes me all night).

Yes, I'll always be bold and be brave.'

So Lil simply sat doing sums in her class,

And nobody, nobody knew

That Lil was a hero, a **swashbuckling** hero,

And all her adventures were true.

# Croc Ahoy!

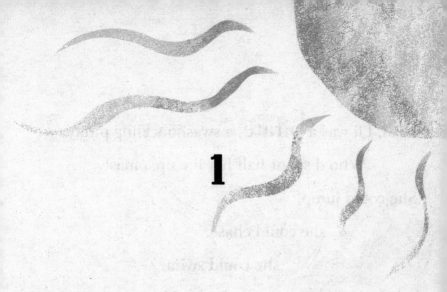

# 1

When Miss Lubber said,

     'Class, it's your sports day today,'

  Nobody, nobody guessed

That in matters of skill there was no one like Lil.

  She was, in fact, simply . . .

            **THE BEST**.

Yes, Lil was a pirate, a swashbuckling pirate,

Who'd spent half her life up a mast.

She could jump,

she could chase,

she could swim,

she could race,

And whatever she did, she did fast.

She could flee through the sea,

she could scale up a tree,

She could sail with the whales all day long.

She could throw, she could catch,

she could win any match,

She was bold, she was brave, she was strong.

So Lil cried, 'Let's go, with a yo, ho, ho!'

When her class all filed off to the park,

Though doing PE wasn't nearly as fun

As battling a

shadowy

shark.

'Now', said Miss Lubber, 'take care on the street.

Make sure that you hold a friend's hand.

Children, this way! Lil, do as I say!

And *why* are you covered in sand?

'Cross at the lights. Walk on the right.

Don't chatter!

Don't natter!

Don't talk!

And was that a child or a bird that I heard?

It sounded a bit like a $^squ^awk!$'

They arrived at the park and Miss Lubber said,

'Kids, The mayor of the city is here!

She'll hand out each prize. Such a lovely surprise!'

The class gave a bored little cheer.

But Lil wasn't listening; she sat near the lake,

Dreaming of trophies she'd win,

When she saw in the grass near the rest of her class

A horrid and hideous grin.

'What a strange-looking puppy', Lil said to herself,

Then she suddenly shuddered in shock.

It wasn't a dog by the side of the log,

But a greedy and villainous . . .

# croc! -

Its eyes were like glass, its teeth were like knives,

Its claws were all poised to attack.

And Lil said, 'I bet that's a foul pirate's pet!

Yes, that scurvy old Stinkbeard's

come back!'

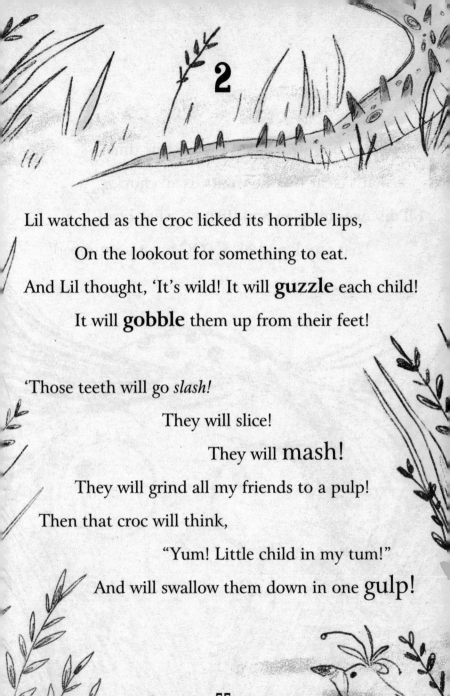

## 2

Lil watched as the croc licked its horrible lips,

On the lookout for something to eat.

And Lil thought, 'It's wild! It will **guzzle** each child!

It will **gobble** them up from their feet!

'Those teeth will go *slash!*

They will slice!

They will **mash!**

They will grind all my friends to a pulp!

Then that croc will think,

"Yum! Little child in my tum!"

And will swallow them down in one gulp!

'Whatever old Stinkbeard is after this time,

It's clear that he wants us all chop-ped.

I'll discover his plan and then do what I can.

That crook and his **croc** must be stopped!'

But just as Lil thought, 'I will follow that croc!'

Miss Lubber yelled, 'Lil, over here!

The races will start and you're here to take part!

At once!

Is that perfectly

clear?

'So these are the rules: stay AWAY from the mud.

Do NOT climb the fences or walls.

Don't cheat. Be fair. And be nice to the mayor.

Now can you remember that all?'


'Maybe,' said Lil. Miss Lubber just frowned,

Saying, 'Come along, children, get set.

On your marks, get ready!

Breathe in!

Get steady!'

When *something* squawked,

Hang on,
not yet!

Children ran.

Children stopped.

Children scratched at their heads.

The race was in full disarray.

'Nice work,' muttered Lil to Carrot the Parrot,

And silently slipped right away.

# 3

A climbing frame stood near the pond in the park,

Looking ever so scary and high.

But Lil thought, 'From there I can spy everywhere.

To climb that's as easy as pie.'

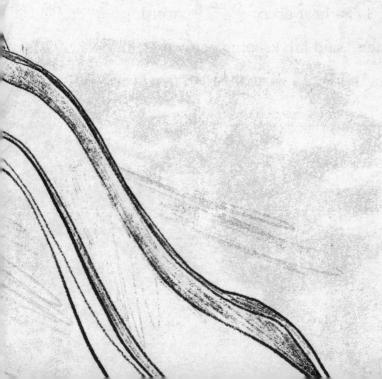

Higher she rose, up, up and up, up,

To the uppermost place she could get.

And there she could see, through the leaves of a tree,

Stinkbeard, in talks with his pet.

'Aha!' chuckled Lil. 'It's clear from up here,

I can hear every whispery word.

I'll listen,' said Lil, keeping perfectly still,

And here's what she then overheard:

'Crockles, my precious, here is our plan:

We'll be brave!

We'll be **brutish** and **bold!**

Gobble those kids with a crunch for your lunch,

Then we'll steal all those trophies of gold.'

'Right, this is war!' spluttered Lil to herself.

'And now let the battle commence!

When Stinkbeard knows that I'm one of his foes

He will flee, if he has any sense!

'Carrot,' she whispered, 'prepare your attack,

And aim for that slimeball's bald head.

STINKBEARD,
WATCH
OUT!

Lil said with a shout,

'I've got you, so tremble in dread!'

Carrot swooped down towards Stinkbeard and Croc,

Closer and closer he flew.

'And now meet your fate,' yelled Lil, 'I can't wait.

Carrot, release all the poo!

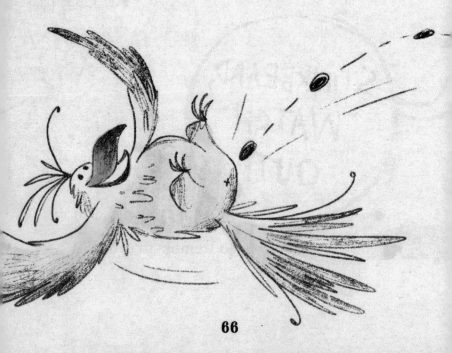

'Stinkbeard, you vermin,' Lil yelled in the breeze,

'You rotten old rascally creature!

You're nothing! You're dust!' Then the wind

gave a gust,

And the poo blew on top of . . .

Lil's teacher!

# 4

'Come here **at once**,' bawled Miss Lubber to Lil,

As poo oozed in streams down her nose.

There was poo on her face and all over the place:

In her hair,

on her bag,

on her clothes!

'Lil,' she said, 'none of your stories this time.

You're in dreadful, yes DREADFUL, disgrace!

I made it quite clear that you couldn't play here.

Now of course you are banned from the race.'

'Humph!' muttered Lil. 'She can say what she likes,

But I'll not be so easily beaten.

If I don't act, then I know for a fact

That my friends will be

chewed up

and eaten.'

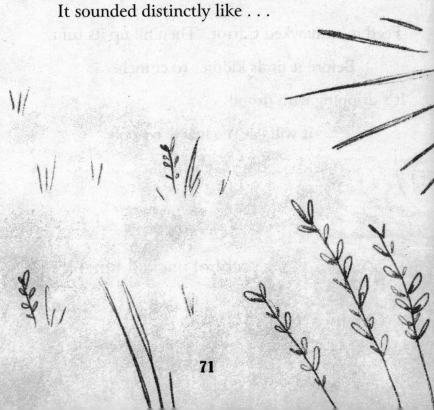

Lil sat all alone as her friends ran around,

Some of them cheering and clapping.

But what was that noise? Not girls and not boys;

It sounded distinctly like . . .

# . . . snapping!

What could Lil do? Where could she go?

She hadn't a moment to think!

There stood the croc!

Lil's heart beat *knock-knock*

As its eye gave a hideous wink.


'Feed it,' squawked Carrot. 'Then fill up its tum,

Before it finds kiddies to crunch.

It's dripping with drool!

It will eat the whole school!

But maybe it likes . . .

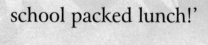

school packed lunch!'

Creeping and crawling, Lil looked for some food;

Her movements were silent and stealthy.

There on the grass was the lunch for her class,

All of it ever so healthy.

There was celery, lettuce and lumpy white cheese,

Tomatoes and brown bread with crusts.

The croc gulped them down,

gave a strange little frown . . .

Then spat them all out in disgust!


Lil looked around for some tastier food;

The mayor's lunch seemed toothsome enough,

With large sausage rolls, crisps in small bowls,

And biscuits and other such stuff.

'It's not really stealing,' Lil said to herself.

'The lives of small kids are at stake!

**Croccy!**' she said, as it reared its large head.

'Come over here – have some cake.'

The croc grinned with greed and ate it all up,

With a slibbery slobbery slurp.

Its belly was filled. It sat looking chilled,

Then it gave an enormous great . . .

BURP!

And just as Lil thought,

    'Good, we're safe here at last!'

    Miss Lubber said, 'What was that sound?'

And she saw, not a claw or a crocodile jaw,

    But ALL of the mess on the ground.


'Oops!' muttered Lil. 'It's a bit of a tip,

    But you always claim tidying's fun.

I'll leave it to you and the others to do.

    And now, er, I think . . .

# I must RUN!'

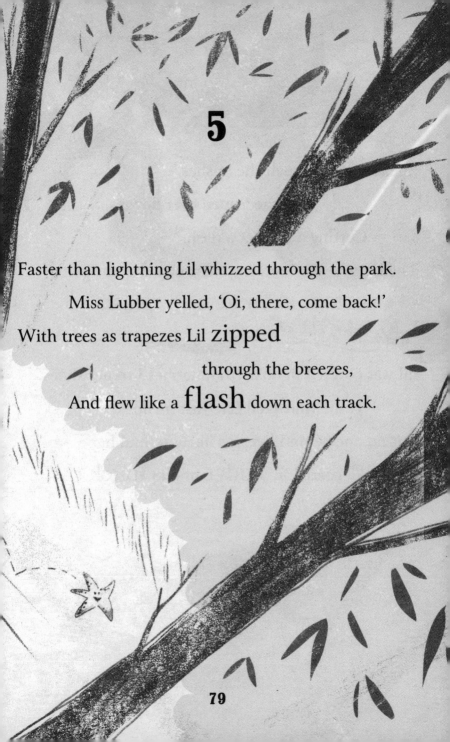

# 5

Faster than lightning Lil whizzed through the park.

Miss Lubber yelled, 'Oi, there, come back!'

With trees as trapezes Lil zipped

through the breezes,

And flew like a flash down each track.

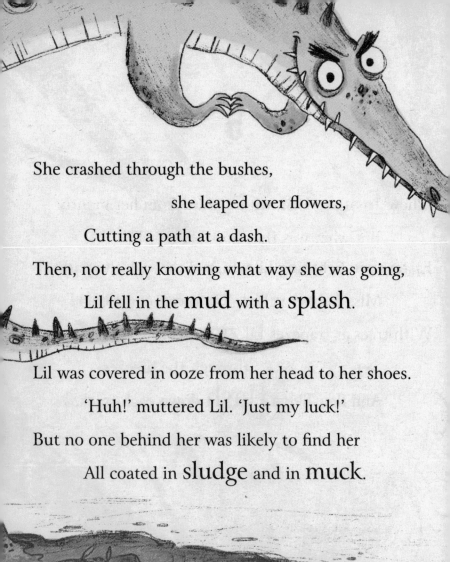

She crashed through the bushes,

she leaped over flowers,

Cutting a path at a dash.

Then, not really knowing what way she was going,

Lil fell in the mud with a splash.

Lil was covered in ooze from her head to her shoes.

'Huh!' muttered Lil. 'Just my luck!'

But no one behind her was likely to find her

All coated in sludge and in muck.

'Phew!' muttered Lil, wiping mud from her mouth.

But what was that horrible growl?

And what was that stench,

over there,

by the bench?

It was Stinkbeard, still out on the prowl!

With a wild 'A-harrr!' Lil leaped from the mud,

Dripping with slippery slime.

'You stinker!

You plotter!

You scumbag!

You rotter!

Beware – I will get you this time!'

Stinkbeard went white. He gave a small yelp.

His knees started shaking in shock.

'A monster!' he cried. 'Oh, help! I must hide!'

And he fled from the park with his croc.


'Shiver me timbers – I've done it!' cheered Lil.

'Now I hope that he never comes back.'

Then Lil said, 'Oh dear! Now Miss Lubber is here!'

And she dived in a nearby sack.

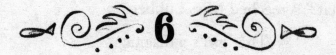

# 6

Sports day was finally reaching an end,

    With only one race left to go.

Who would come first? Who would be worst?

    Who would be fast, and who slow?

The whistle went off. The children began

    Jumping in sacks up the hill.

But whose was that sack at the front of the track?

    Of course! Yes, the winner was . . .

Lil!

'What?' screeched Miss Lubber.

'That girl's a disgrace,

Who never behaves as she's told.

She's a naughty young child, she's totally **wild**.

Lil doesn't **deserve** to win gold.'

'I can see,' said the mayor,

      'that she's covered in muck,

    But I'm sure she was just having fun.

This girl was the best, she beat all the rest,

    So she gets the prize.

                      Yes, she's won.'

'Oo-arrr!' whispered Lil to her trusty old parrot.

'It seems that I've got us some booty.

It's the best bit of bounty in all of the county,

Isn't it, Carrot, me beauty?'

Then Lil simply went back to school with her class,

And nobody, nobody knew

That Lil was a **hero**, a swashbuckling hero,

And all her adventures were **true**.

# The Jewel Thief

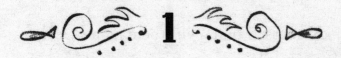

Normaltown School was a dull sort of place.

Nothing went on all day L O N G .

'It's always the same,' the children complained,

But, actually, there they were wrong . . .

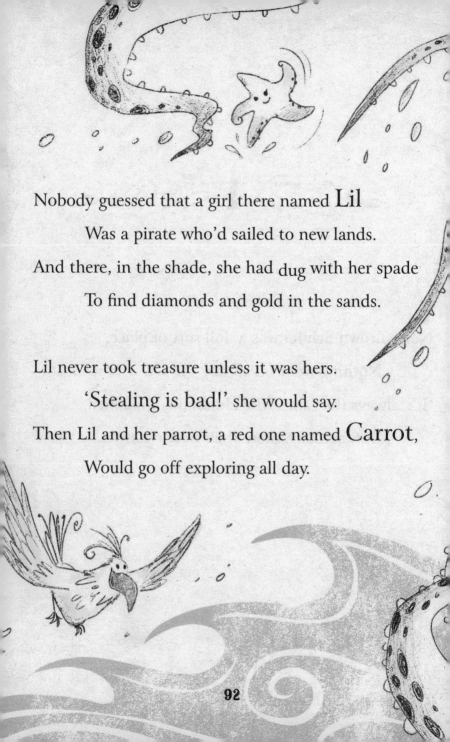

Nobody guessed that a girl there named Lil

Was a pirate who'd sailed to new lands.

And there, in the shade, she had dug with her spade

To find diamonds and gold in the sands.

Lil never took treasure unless it was hers.

'Stealing is bad!' she would say.

Then Lil and her parrot, a red one named Carrot,

Would go off exploring all day.

But if danger appeared in the winds and the waves,

Then Lil was as **bold** as could be.

She tackled big squid in the depths where they hid.

'Nothing,' she'd say, 'can scare ME!'

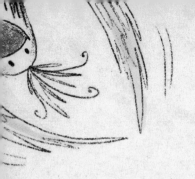

Yet even a pirate must learn how to read,

So that is why Lil sat in class.

But she daydreamed of whales,

and lightning-lashed gales,

And waters that glimmered like glass.

Miss Lubber, her teacher, would say to her, 'Lil!

Why is there sand on your chair?

Look at your shirt! It's covered in dirt,

And there's seaweed all over your hair!'

Then one day Miss Lubber said,

'Class, I've got news.'

'Oooh!' said the children. 'What is it?'

'Today,' said Miss Lubber, 'we'll all go away

On a wonderful, interesting visit.'

'This museum,' she said, 'will be ever so fun.

It's an **excellent** place for a trip.

We'll see famous old art, and the very best part

Is a hundred-and-ten-year-old ship.'

MUSEUM THIS WAY

'Ahoy!' shouted Lil. 'I know all about boats!'

But Miss Lubber just said, 'Come along.

Now, Lil, please be good and behave as you should,

And nothing at all will go wrong.'

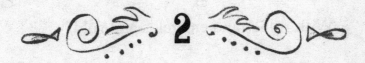

## 2

The museum was huge. 'Carrot,' said Lil,

'Just look at this place – it's so cool!'

But Miss Lubber said, 'Lil, I have told you:

## STAND STILL.

Now, children, remember this rule:

'The stuff in museums is valuable art;

Just think of the millions it cost.

No touching, no reaching, no squealing or screeching,

And don't run around or get lost.'

'All of this stuff is like treasure,' thought Lil.

'It's really expensive and old.

And look! Here's a ring that belonged to a king,

With rubies and emeralds and gold.'

But the children said,

      'Miss, it's so BORING in here.

    Where's that big ship, like you said?'

'Over here,' said Miss Lubber, and everyone cheered

    As they ran through the doors straight ahead.

Miss Lubber was telling the class to be good.

'Listen,' she said, 'and don't talk.

We LEARN when we're here – is that perfectly clear?

But wait . . . What on earth was that squawk?'

'Shhh,' whispered Lil. 'Carrot, be good!

I told you – be quiet, don't chatter!

Don't flutter, don't speak, don't flap and don't shriek.

But hang on a sec – what's the matter?'

Then all of a sudden Lil let out a gaSp,

As she stroked her pet bird in her bag.

For right on the tip of the mast of the ship

Was Stinkbeard's
filthy old
FLAG!

# 3

Stinkbeard was feared by all pirating folks.

He'd always, yes, *always* been mean.

There were bugs in his beard and his face was

all smeared

With the mouldiest food ever seen.

'Whatever old Stinkbeard is up to,' thought Lil,

'It's bound to be something that's **bad**.

He's always invading and looting and raiding;

He's foul, he's revolting, he's mad!'

'Miss Lubber!' Lil called. 'Ahoy, over here!'

But her teacher said, 'Lil, pay attention.

I've told you: don't shout when we're out and about,

Or else I will give you detention.

'Now hurry up, class – it's time for your snack.

 We'll all sit and eat it outside.'

But Lil muttered, 'No, I'm not going to go.

 Quickly now, Carrot, let's hide!'


A large wooden barrel was right by the ship.

 Lil said, 'Let's spy from in there.

Stinkbeard won't know that we're here. Yo ho ho!

 We'll JUMP OUT and give him a scare!'

'Won't Stinkbeard be shocked by my plan?' giggled Lil.

'But wait! Are those footsteps I hear?

They're *clop-clop-clop clopping*, and still they're

not stopping,

Oh no! They sound dangerously near!'

Then the barrel was tipping, and sliding and slipping,
And starting to swing and to sway;
'What's happening?' thought Lil. 'We're going downhill!'
The barrel was rolling away.

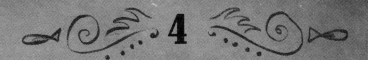

# 4

Down, down Lil rolled, yelling, 'Stinkbeard, you rat!

I will get you for this, just you see!

You revolting old crab! You can snatch, you can grab,

But you'll not make a prisoner of ME!'

The barrel slowed down. Lil tried to climb out,

But the lid was locked shut with a snap.

And a voice said, 'I WILL take you prisoner, young Lil!

Aharrrr! Now you're caught in my trap.'

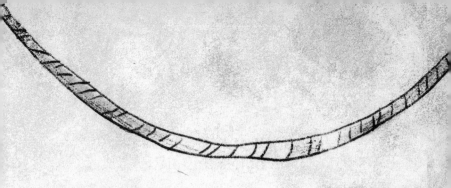

Lil bashed on the lid with a *bang, bang, bang, CLANG!*

But Stinkbeard just snorted and laughed.

'I won't let you go and escape, no, no, no!

You'll never get out – I'm not daft!'

'Later today I will burgle this place,

And grab an exhibit or two.

I'll steal that old ring that belonged to a king,

And there's nothing at all you can do.'

'Carrot,' said Lil as the minutes ticked by,

'I think Stinkbeard's having a kip.

His snoring's like THUNDER. Now, listen, I wonder . . .

Perhaps we can give him the slip.'

She whispered some words
        in her pet parrot's ear,
Then Carrot pecked hard at the lid.
The holes grew and grew
        till the lid broke in two,
And out Lil and Carrot both slid.

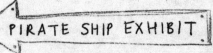

PIRATE SHIP EXHIBIT

OLD KING'S JEWELS

'Stinkbeard's a slimy old thief!' muttered Lil.

'Carrot, we must stop this crime!

I'm sure that we can and I've thought of a plan,

But hurry – there isn't much time!'

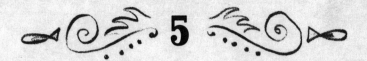

In the very next room was a case of old clothes

That were once worn by little princesses.

There were shoes, there were boots, there were coats,
there were suits,

And a dozen or so frilly dresses.

She pulled on a dress saying, 'Here's our disguise.

Listen now, Carrot, my mate.

We'll be statues,' said Lil. 'We must just keep still,

And all we can do now is w a i t .'

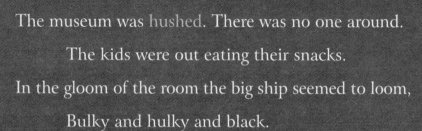

The museum was hushed. There was no one around.

   The kids were out eating their snacks.

In the gloom of the room the big ship seemed to loom,

   Bulky and hulky and black.

But wait! What was that? A flickering light?

   Someone had just lit a match.

And then there appeared a revolting big beard

   As Stinkbeard crawled out of a hatch.

The pirate crept to the edge of the ship,

And swung himself over the deck.

He looked all around, then said,

'Wait! What's that sound?

There's somebody in here. Oh heck!'

'It's only a statue!' said Stinkbeard. 'Oh phew!

For a moment I thought it was real!

And a stupid stuffed bird? Hee hee, how absurd!

Aharrrr! Now I'll go off and steal.'

The lock on the case was quite easy to pick.

'Oh ho!' Stinkbeard said. 'I'm the best.'

But just as he grabbed at the king's ruby ring,

A voice squawked,

'You're under arrest!'

# 6

'Heeeeeelp!' Stinkbeard shouted.

'That parrot just spoke.

But how can a stuffed parrot talk?

And that statue is moving towards me,' he screeched.

'What's happening? A statue can't walk!

'They're demons! They're devils! They're ghosties!

They're ghouls!

They're coming to get me!' he said.

'That bird bit my bum! I WANT MY MUM!'

And quickly he turned and he fled.

'After him, Carrot!' the 'statue' cried out.

'Tickle him, quick, with your wing.

We'll hunt him and chase him! We'll hound him

and race him!

We must make him drop that old ring!'


They zipped and they zoomed through the halls

and the rooms,

Whizzing along at top speed.

They darted and dashed in a blur and a flash,

But Stinkbeard was still in the lead.

'STOP!' yelled the guards as they woke

from their snooze.

'Hey, what on earth's going on?'

And puffing and panting they joined in the chase,

But Stinkbeard seemed to have gone.

'You scumbag!' yelled Lil. 'You're scared – is that it?

Is that why you've just disappeared?'

Then she stepped on a rug, but it gave a small tug,

And she came face to face with . . . a beard!

'Arrrrrr!' Stinkbeard cried. 'You'll never stop *me*!

I've grabbed you and nabbed you at last.

This treasure's all mine, you revolting young swine!'

But Lil simply said, 'Not so fast!'

# 7

Lil whipped out the laces from both of her shoes,

    Then tied Stinkbeard's legs good and fast.

She tied his hands too, then she cried out, 'Woo hoo!

    I've finally caught you at last!'

'Huh!' Stinkbeard said. 'I'll soon get away,'

    But he started to stumble and slip,

Then he tumbled – *ker-thwack* – fell smack on his back,

    And the ring slithered out of his grip.

PA-DOING

The laces went *SNAP*, and off Stinkbeard ran,

Yelling, 'Ha! I am out of this place!'

Then Lil grabbed the ring that belonged to a king,

And she put it right back in its case.

Then all of a sudden Miss Lubber came up,

And her voice was a horrible hiss.

'All of this mess! You made it, I guess?

Yes, WHAT is the meaning of THIS?'

Lil tried to explain, but Miss Lubber said, 'Child,

That's the silliest thing that I've heard!

A pirating crook and a ring that he took?

I don't believe one single word!'

'Really!' thought Lil as the class all marched home.

'Teachers are always unfair!

I acted in time to prevent a huge crime,

But Miss Lubber – she just doesn't care!'


So Lil got in trouble at school yet again,

And nobody, nobody knew

That Lil was a hero, a swashbuckling hero,

And all her adventures were true.

# Party, Me Hearty!

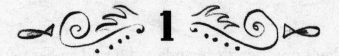

**1**

Lil and her parrot were strolling along

When Lil whispered,

'Carrot, me hearty,

Don't make a sound and don't flip-flap around.

Remember,

we're off to Bill's **PARTY.'**

'Today's my friend's birthday,' Lil said to her pet.

    'We must behave nicely, all right?

His mum will be there, so we'll have to take care

    To be ever so good and polite.'

But Lil sighed to herself as she walked past the shops,

    'I'd rather be out on the waves.

I'd dive in the sea and catch fish for my tea,

    Then roast it on campfires in caves.

'A party's not nearly exciting enough;

    You just sit around playing games.

There aren't coral reefs, or bad pirate chiefs,

    Or sea-monsters breathing out flames.'

She st<sup>o</sup>m<sub>p</sub><sup>e</sup>d past the park, she st<sup>a</sup>m<sub>p</sub><sup>e</sup>d past her school,

And on to her friend's big front door.

But then she said, 'Wait! What's this by the gate?

A poster? And what is it for?'

STOLEN:
OLD COINS PRICED
AT MILLIONS OF POUNDS,
A GLITTERING GLIMMERING
HOARD.
THEIR OWNERS CONSIDERED
AND THEY MUST BE
RETURNED.
FIND THEM AND CLAIM
A REWARD.

*Stolen: old coins priced at millions of pounds,*

    *A glittering, glimmering hoard.*

*Their owner's concerned and they must be returned.*

    *Find them and claim a reward.*

'Stinkbeard!' said Lil. 'I bet it was him!

    That wicked old pirating chief!

We'll find where that brute has concealed all this loot,

    And then we will catch that foul thief!'

## 2

Lil knocked on the door and a woman appeared

Looking terribly tidy and neat.

She peered down her nose at Lil's scruffy clothes,

Then barked, 'Come inside. Wipe your feet.'

143

'I'm Bill's mother,' she said in a grim sort of voice.

'You're one of his friends then, I guess?

The party's in here, but I must make this clear:

No shouting, and don't make a mess.'

'Oh dear,' whispered Lil to the bird in her bag.

'Isn't she horribly snooty?

But we still must be good and behave as we should,

So come along, Carrot, me beauty.'

The rest of Bill's friends had already arrived.

They saw Lil and said, 'Oh, hello!'

Bill's mum gave a glare and a mean sort of stare

When Lil replied, 'Hey! Yo ho ho!'

'Children, it's time for some games,' said Bill's mum.

'But listen to me, girls and boys.

No jumping, no bumping, and please, kids,

no thumping.

Be gentle, and not too much noise.'

146

'Huh!' muttered Lil, as Carrot hopped off.

'It's as boring as boring could be!'

And she thought of the hoard and

the promised reward.

'Where,' murmured Lil,

'could it be?'

Then all of a sudden her parrot returned,

And he dropped something –

PLOP

– in her lap.

'Look what I found,'

Carrot squawked, 'on the ground.'

'Oh!' muttered Lil.

'It's a map!

'What does it say? The ink is all smudged.

But one thing is perfectly clear:

This map leaves no doubt that old Stinkbeard's about,

And the coins that he stole must be near.'

# 3

When no one was looking Lil slipped off outside.

'Carrot!' she said. 'Come and look!

Footprints, I think, and they pong! Yes, they stink!

I bet they belong to that crook!'

'But whose prints are these? Not human at all . . .

Right over here, by this rock.

It's not fluffy paws,

but something with claws –

It must be old Stinkbeard's

pet **CROC**!'

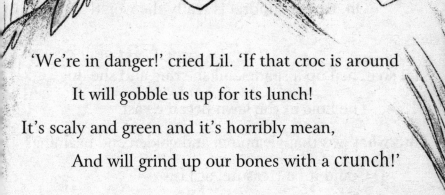

'We're in danger!' cried Lil. 'If that croc is around

It will gobble us up for its lunch!

It's scaly and green and it's horribly mean,

And will grind up our bones with a crunch!'


'Stinkbeard, I know that you're hiding,' called Lil.

'Show me your face, if you dare!'

And she looked all around, but there wasn't a sound;

Stinkbeard, it seemed, wasn't there.

'That scumbag will come for the treasure,' said Lil,

    'But we'll have to make sure we're there first.

Or else he'll come back and he's sure to attack.

    Oh, that scoundrel is really the worst!'


Lil snatched up a spade and she dug and she dug.

    The hole in the lawn became vast.

But what was that gleaming, and golden and beaming?

    Could it be treasure, at last?

'The coins!' shouted Lil. 'I know that they are!'

And she started to scrape off the mud.

'We've done it!' cried Lil, and turned

cartwheels, until . . .

Footsteps came up –

*thud, thud, THUD!*

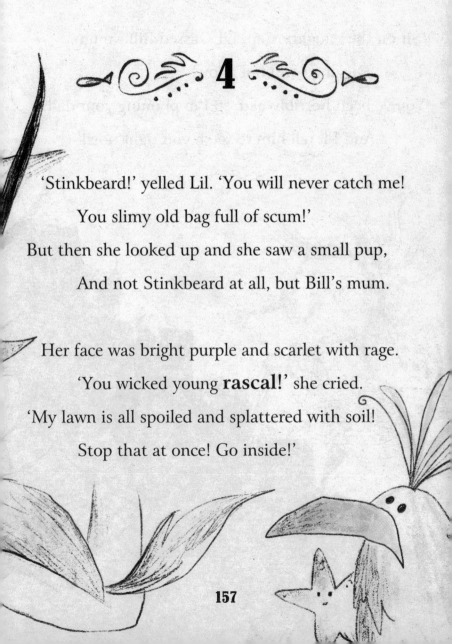

# 4

'Stinkbeard!' yelled Lil. 'You will never catch me!

You slimy old bag full of scum!'

But then she looked up and she saw a small pup,

And not Stinkbeard at all, but Bill's mum.


Her face was bright purple and scarlet with rage.

'You wicked young **rascal!**' she cried.

'My lawn is all spoiled and splattered with soil!

Stop that at once! Go inside!'

'Sit on the naughty step, Lil,' hissed Bill's mum.

'Digging I will not allow!

You've been horribly bad, so I'm phoning your dad,

And I'll tell him to fetch you right now!'

'That beast will come back for the treasure,' thought Lil,

'And nobody else even cares!

But that scoundrel will see

that a step won't stop ME!

But hang on – what's that on the stairs?'

'Seaweedy slime!' Lil said to herself.

'Right on each step – a whole trail.

And there at the top, where it comes to a stop,

Is the tip of a **scaly green tail!**'

Lil leaped up the stairs, three at a time,

And gave the most ear-splitting yell.

'Stinkbeard, I bet you I'm going to get you!

And may I inform you – you smell.'

Lil searched in the bedrooms; she peered under beds,

In wardrobes and drawers of all sorts.

But the tail and the beard had just disappeared.

'Perhaps in the bathroom?' Lil thought.

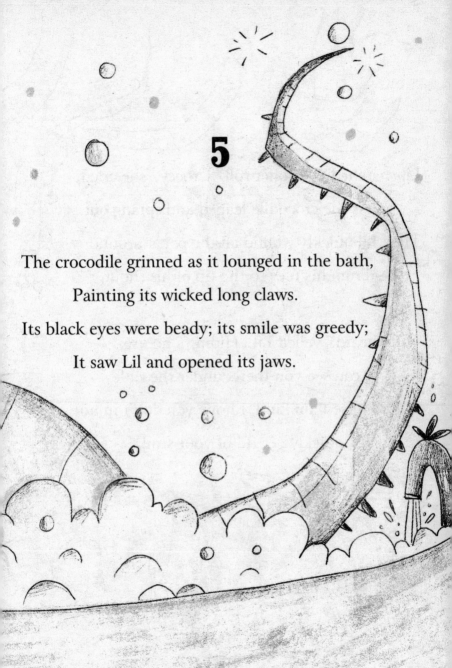

**5**

The crocodile grinned as it lounged in the bath,

Painting its wicked long claws.

Its black eyes were beady; its smile was greedy;

It saw Lil and opened its jaws.

Lil snatched at a toilet roll. 'Croccy,' she cried,

As the crocodile leaped and sprang out.

Then Lil quickly wound all the paper around

From his toes to the tip of his snout.


'Stinkbeard!' yelled Lil. 'Hiding's no use.

I can see you there, under the sink.

But because I am kind, I hope you don't mind

If I quickly get rid of your stink.'

A big can of shaving cream stood on the floor.

Lil grabbed it and said, 'Now, take that!'

The foam spurted out in a huge frothy spout,

And landed on Stinkbeard –

**kerSPLAT**!

'And now you could do

with a rinse,' shouted Lil,

Giving Stinkbeard a sweet little grin.

And she turned on the shower

with a switch marked

**FULL POWER** . . .

Just as Bill's mother walked in!

The woman was soaking; her clothes were all wet;
> On her face was a furious scowl.
'Oops,' muttered Lil. 'I'm sorry, but still,
> It's easily dried – have a towel.'

Lil slid down the banister, back to her friends,
> Who were all standing staring below.
'I'll be back in a tick,' said Lil. 'I'll be quick,
> But I need to find treasure, yo ho!'

# 6

Carrot was waiting for Lil in a tree.

He fluttered down fast in a flurry.

'To the treasure!' Lil cried as she darted outside.

'We'll stop that old brute if we hurry!'

But then she glanced up at a window above.

'A ladder?' Lil said with a frown.

It swayed and it shook, and *there* was the crook!

Stinkbeard was clambering down!

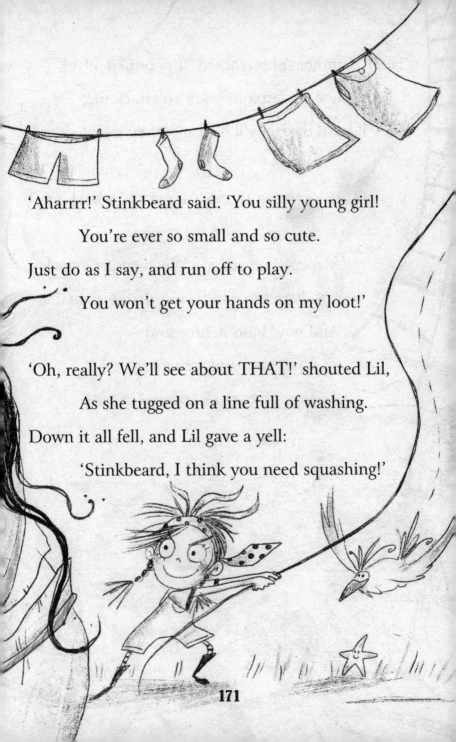

'Aharrrr!' Stinkbeard said. 'You silly young girl!

You're ever so small and so cute.

Just do as I say, and run off to play.

You won't get your hands on my loot!'

'Oh, really? We'll see about THAT!' shouted Lil,

As she tugged on a line full of washing.

Down it all fell, and Lil gave a yell:

'Stinkbeard, I think you need squashing!'

'Help!' Stinkbeard screamed. 'I'm buried alive!

These underpants want to attack me!

They'll bosh me, they'll beat me, they might even

eat me!

They're trying to thwack me and whack me!'

'Croccy!' he yelled. 'We must get away!

There seem to be murderous pants!

And now I am itching and

scratching and scritching.

Arrrrrr! They're all covered in ants!'

'Yo HO!' muttered Lil as Stinkbeard ran off.

'And now for the treasure – come on!'

So she dug, but then said, with a tremble of dread,

'Carrot, the treasure has gone!'

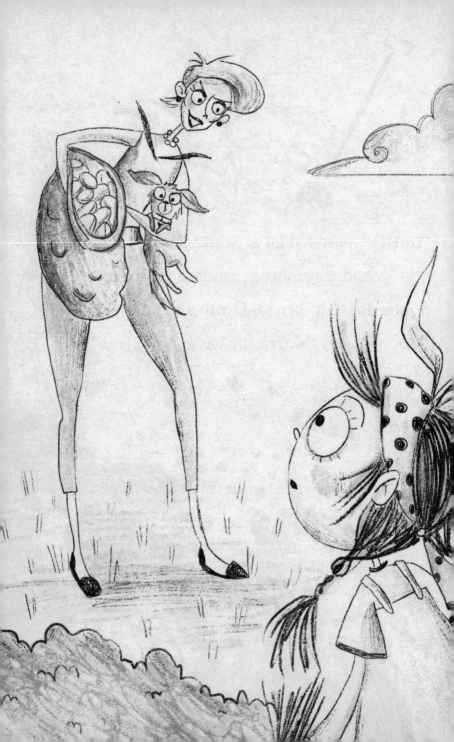

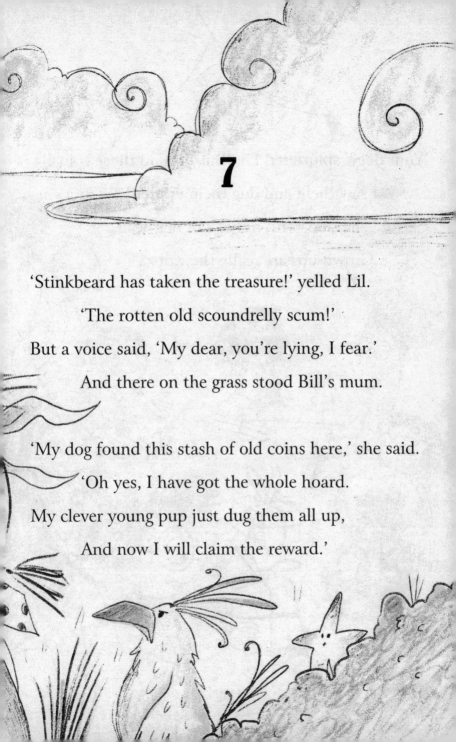

# 7

'Stinkbeard has taken the treasure!' yelled Lil.

'The rotten old scoundrelly scum!'

But a voice said, 'My dear, you're lying, I fear.'

And there on the grass stood Bill's mum.

'My dog found this stash of old coins here,' she said.

'Oh yes, I have got the whole hoard.

My clever young pup just dug them all up,

And now I will claim the reward.'

'Your dog?' spluttered Lil. 'But *I* found those coins!

I saw them and dug them up first!

Carrot,' she said, with a shake of her head,

'Grown-ups are really the worst!'

Lil went inside. Her friends were still there,

   All of them happily playing.

'Huh!' Lil declared as she angrily glared.

   'This place is no fun. I'm not staying!'

But passing the kitchen Lil looked and she saw

The food for the party – a feast!

'Carrot, tuck in!' said Lil with a grin.

'We both deserve this much at least!'


'Look, there are coins made of chocolate,' said Lil,

And Carrot squawked, 'Pieces of eight!'

Then he bit a big slice of something else nice,

And said to Lil, 'Pizzas are great!'

So Lil went back home from the party that day,

And nobody, nobody knew,

That Lil was a pirate, a fearless young pirate,

And all her adventures were true.

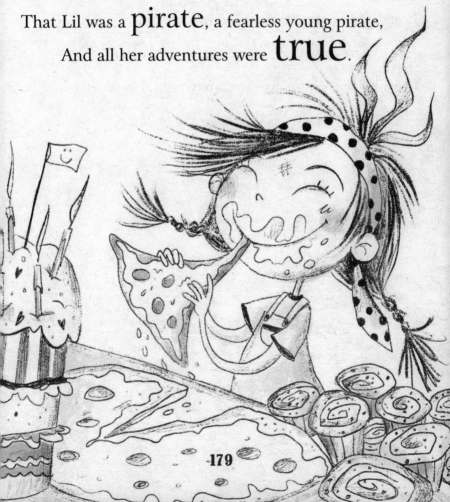

# About the Author

Elli Woollard started writing stories after an embarrassing incident in which her youngest son broke Michael Rosen's glasses! In addition to picture books, she also writes children's poems and stories. Elli's picture books with Macmillan include *The Giant of Jum*, *The Dragon and the Nibblesome Knight* and *The Great Gran Plan*. She has also retold Rudyard Kipling's *Just So Stories* in rhyme and created the two Swashbuckle Lil books for young readers. Elli lives in London with her four children, her husband and two guinea pigs.

# About the Illustrator

Laura Ellen Anderson has been drawing ever since she can remember. She is the accomplished illustrator of many picture books and young-fiction series, including *Witch Wars*, *My Brother Is a Superhero* and the Evil Emperor Penguin comic strip for *The Phoenix*. Her first author-illustrator picture book, *I Don't Want Curly Hair*, was published in 2017 and her debut young-fiction series, Amelia Fang, is off to a fangtastic start!

# More fun from
# ELLI WOOLLARD
*for younger readers*